Will You Be My Valenswine?

Teresa Bateman

ILLUSTRATED BY

Kristina Stephenson

ALBERT WHITMAN & COMPANY, MORTON GROVE, ILLINOIS

Library of Congress Cataloging-in-Publication Data

Bateman, Teresa.
Will you be my valenswine? / written by Teresa Bateman ; illustrated by
Kristina Stephenson.
p. cm.
Summary: A sad piglet named Polly searches the pasture, forest, and barnyard
for someone to love her, only to discover that her valenswine has been there all along.
ISBN 10: 0-8075-9196-3 (paperback) ISBN 13: 978-0-8075-9196-3 (paperback)
ISBN 10: 0-8075-9195-5 (hardcover) ISBN 13: 978-0-8075-9195-6 (hardcover)
[1. Valentines—Fiction. 2. Pigs—Fiction. 3. Mother and child—Fiction. 4. Stories in rhyme.]
I. Stephenson, Kristina, ill. II. Title.
PZ8.3.B314Wi 2005 [E]—dc22 2005001964

Text copyright © 2005 by Teresa Bateman.
Illustrations copyright © 2005 by Kristina Stephenson.
Published in 2005 by Albert Whitman & Company,
6340 Oakton Street, Morton Grove, Illinois 60053-2723.
Published simultaneously in Canada by Fitzhenry & Whiteside, Markham, Ontario.

Printed in the United States.
10 9 8 7 6 5 4 3 2

The design is by Carol Gildar and Kristina Stephenson.

For more information about Albert Whitman & Company,
please visit our web site at www.albertwhitman.com.

To my mother, who easily fulfills all
Polly's prerequisites.—T.B.

For Rebecca Outterside and Bethany George,
because they love pigs.—K.S.

On Valentine's Day, a little piggy
began to mope and whine.
For that pouting pig, named Polly,
didn't have a valenswine.

While the stallion had his mare,
and even rams said, "I love ewe,"
Polly thought she had no one
to send hearts and flowers to.

She went slumping 'round the pigpen
with a bad case of the grumps,
till her mother asked her gently,
"Why are you down in the dumps?"

"I have no valenswine," she sighed.
"I just want somebody sweet.
Someone with a loving voice
to make me feel complete.
I need a valenswine to feel
all warm and full inside."

She longed to have a valenswine
so much she nearly cried.

"You need fresh air," her mother said.
"Go out and think things through.
I'm sure you'll see, if given time,
that someone here loves you."

Polly puttered in the pasture,
sniffing sadly through her snout.
Then she sniffed again. "That's something sweet!"
She quickly turned about.

There were roses twining on the fence.
"Oh, Rose, you are divine.
So please tell me that you will be
my one true valenswine."

But the roses didn't say a word
to answer Polly's call.
Her piglet heart was broken.
She had no one at all.

Her mother gave that pig a squeeze.
"Oh, Polly, please don't pout.
Just look around—there's someone here
who loves you, tail to snout."

Polly headed to the forest,
where she heard a sparrow's song.
"How pretty," Polly said. "This time
I know I can't be wrong!"

"You have a lilting, loving voice.
You make the morning shine.
So tell me, Sparrow, that you'll be
my one true valenswine."

The bird just kept on singing.
She ignored that piglet's call.
Poor Polly's heart was broken—
she had no one at all.

"Oh, piddle," said her mother,
giving Polly a quick pat.
"I think you'll find that someone here
can love you more than that."

Polly wandered through the barnyard,
spying fresh slop in the trough.
She slurped and gobbled, gulped and chomped,
then licked the drippings off.

She felt all warm and full inside.
"Oh, Slop, I love to dine.
So please tell me that you will be
my one true valenswine."

The slop just lay there, silent.
It ignored that piglet's call.
Poor Polly's heart was broken—
she had no one at all!

Her mother came and kissed her.
Polly cuddled up, then sighed.
"I love you," said her mother.
Polly felt all warm inside.

Her mother's voice was loving,
and her mother's words were sweet.
Her smile made Polly warm and full.
Her love made her complete.

"Oh, Mother!" piglet Polly said.
"Please say that you'll be mine.
Right now I see you are, for me,
the perfect valenswine!"

Her mother smiled as Polly yawned.
They snuggled by their stall.
For Polly's big discovery
was no surprise at all!